# The Bear and the Mountain

Warren Publishing House, Inc.

Warren Publishing House, Inc., P.O. Box 2250, Everett, WA 98203, 1-800-334-4769.

Printed in Hong Kong by Mandarin Offset.
First Edition   10  9  8  7  6  5  4  3  2  1

Warren, Jean 1940-
    The bear and the mountain / by Jean Warren ; illustrated by Judy Shimono ; activity illustrations by Barbara Tourtillotte. — 1st ed.
        p.      cm.
    Summary: A lonely mountain finds happiness when a little brown bear comes to spend the summer with him. Includes songs and activities about bears and mountains.

    ISBN 0-911019-98-7 (pbk.): $5.95

    [1. Mountains—Fiction.  2. Bears—Fiction.  3. Friendship—Fiction.  4. Stories in rhyme.  5. Handicraft.]  I. Shimono, Judy, ill.  II. Tourtillotte, Barb, 1955- ill.  III. Title.
PZ8.3.W2459Be  1994
[E]—dc20                                                          93-38781
                                                                 CIP
                                                                 AC

Warren Publishing House, Inc. would like to acknowledge the following activity contributors:

Terri Crosbie, Oldwick, NJ
Ellen Javernick, Loveland, CO
Joyce Marshall, Whitby, Ontario, Canada
Judith McNitt, Adrian, MI
Carla Cotter Skjong, Tyler, MN
Nancy Windes, Denver, CO

# The Bear and the Mountain

## By Jean Warren

Illustrated by Judy Shimono

There once was a mountain,
So big and so tall,
Who lived all alone
With no friends at all.

He smiled at the planes
High in the sky.
But none of them stopped,
They just flew on by.

All through the winter
He was covered with snow.
Then during the summer,
Wild flowers would grow.

He often saw people,
Who came just to play.
But none of them ever
Wanted to stay.

They all were too busy,
Too much on the go.
Up they would climb
Then down they would flow.

Then one fine day
Something panted and sighed,
As it huffed and puffed
Up the mountain's side.

Slowly up the mountain
Came a little brown bear,
Wearing wild flowers
In her soft, fuzzy hair.

"Hello, Big Mountain!
How do you do?
May I please spend
The summer with you?"

"Of course!" said the mountain.
"It will be fun.
Run all you like
On my tummy-tum-tum."

Little Bear was happy.
The mountain was, too.
Having a friend
Was something quite new.

Little Bear would race
Up the mountain's side.
Then down she would roll
And slip and slide.

All through the summer
Their friendship grew.
But then one day
The cold winds blew.

Now Little Bear knew
That she had to go
Before the mountain
Was covered with snow.

"Please don't go!"
The mountain cried.
"I'll make a safe place
Where you can hide."

He rumbled and rolled,
Then cupped his arm
To make a warm cave,
Safe from all harm.

Now Little Bear
Had a cozy new home.
And never again
Would she have to roam.

Let the snow come—
She didn't care.
She had a home
Just right for a bear.

The bear and the mountain
Were a sight to see,
Together as friends,
Living happily.

# A Note to Parents and Teachers

The activities in this book have been written so that children in first, second, and third grade can follow most of the directions with minimal adult help. The activities are also appropriate for 3- to 5-year-old children, who can easily do the suggested activities with your help.

You may also wish to extend the learning opportunities in this book by discussing mountains and how they were formed and the seasons and how they affect the mountains.

Outings with children, whether a drive up a mountain or a walk through the park, offer many learning experiences. Children love to look for opposites in any new situation (the snow is cold; my mittens are warm), and they can also be great size detectives (the tree is big; the chipmunk is small). Looking for different colors and types of wildflowers can also be fun.

Children learn so much better when they can express their ideas and feelings through age-appropriate activities. We know you'll enjoy seeing your children's eyes light up when you extend a story with fun, related activities.

# Storytime Fun

## The Bears Are Walking

Sung to: "When Johnny Comes
Marching Home"

The bears are walking

Through the woods

Today, today.

The bears are walking

Through the woods

To eat and play.

They catch some fish

And eat them too.

They munch on berries,

Quite a few.

Then they run around

And climb a tree or two.

*Jean Warren*

## Little Bear

Sung to: "Frere Jacques"

Are you sleeping, are you sleeping,

Little bear, little bear?

You will sleep all winter,

Through the cold, cold winter,

Little bear, little bear.

Are you sleeping, are you sleeping,

Little bear, little bear?

You will wake in springtime,

In the warm, warm springtime,

Little bear, little bear.

*Carla Cotter Skjong*

## Time for Sleeping
Sung to: "Sing a Song of Sixpence"

Now it's time for sleeping,

The bears go in their caves.

Keeping warm and cozy,

Time for lazy days.

When the snow is gone

And the sun comes out to play,

The bears will wake up from their sleep

And then go on their way.

*Terri Crosbie*

## Bears Are Sleeping
Sung to: "Frere Jacques"

Bears are sleeping,

Bears are sleeping,

In their lairs

In their lairs.

Soon it will be springtime,

Soon it will be springtime.

Wake up, bears,

Wake up, bears!

*Joyce Marshall*

## The Bear

Here is a cave.
Inside is a bear.
Now he comes out
To get some fresh air.

He stays out all summer
In sunshine and heat.
He hunts in the forest
For berries to eat.

When snow starts to fall,
He hurries inside
His warm little cave
Where he will hide.

Snow covers the cave
Like a fluffy white rug.
Inside the bear sleeps,
All cozy and snug.

*Author Unknown*

## A Little Brown Bear

A little brown bear
Went in search of some honey.
Isn't it funny,
A bear wanting honey?

He sniffed at the breeze
And he listened for bees.
And would you believe it,
He even climbed trees!

*Adapted Traditional*

# FUZZY BEARS

*Give these bears their warm winter coats!*

1.

2.

3.

**YOU WILL NEED**
- scissors
- brown construction paper
- paintbrush
- glue
- sawdust

**1.** Use scissors to cut a bear shape out of brown construction paper.

**2.** Use a paintbrush to spread glue all over the bear shape.

**3.** Give your bear a winter coat by sprinkling some sawdust on top of the glue.

**FOR MORE FUN**
- Instead of sprinkling sawdust on your bear shape, sprinkle on used tea leaves or coffee grounds that have been rinsed and dried.

- Glue small dried flowers in your bear's hair.

# TEDDY-BEAR PUPPETS

*Turn a plain brown lunch sack into a puppet!*

1–3.

4.

## YOU WILL NEED
- scissors
- construction paper
- glue
- brown lunch sacks

**1.** Use scissors to cut bear facial features out of construction paper.

**2.** Glue the facial features to the bottom of a paper lunch sack to create a bear face (see picture above).

**3.** Cut two bear ear shapes out of construction paper.

**4.** Glue on the ear shapes above the face on your puppet.

## FOR MORE FUN
- Instead of using lunch sacks to make your Teddy-Bear Puppets, use large grocery sacks.

- Make a small puppet, a medium-sized puppet, and a large puppet and use them to act out the story "Goldilocks and the Three Bears."

# FELT BEARS

*Make a fuzzy bear out of a piece of felt!*

1.

2.

3.

## YOU WILL NEED
- brown felt
- paintbrush
- glue
- small paper plate
- two black buttons
- red button
- black yarn

**1.** Tear brown felt into tiny pieces. Keep tearing the pieces until the felt is fuzzy and furlike.

**2.** Use a paintbrush to spread glue all over a small paper plate. Then sprinkle on the felt "fur."

**3.** Glue on two black buttons for eyes, a red button for a nose, two brown felt ears, and make a mouth with black yarn.

## FOR MORE FUN
- Instead of tearing apart a piece of felt, use scissors to cut brown yarn into tiny pieces of "fur."

- To make a polar bear, tear apart a piece of white felt and glue the fuzz onto a paper plate.

# PAPER FLOWERS

*Make a winter garden bloom!*

1–4.

5–6.

## YOU WILL NEED

- scissors
- a 5 ½-by-8 ½-inch piece of construction paper
- tape

**1.** Fold a 5 ½-by-8 ½-inch piece of construction paper in half crosswise.

**2.** Fold the open edges of the construction paper up about an inch, then fold it back down so a crease shows.

**3.** Make about five cuts through the folded end and down to the crease you made in step 2.

**4.** Pull the sections apart and curl the paper into a circle.

**5.** Tape the ends together to form a large flower.

## FOR MORE FUN

- Make larger Paper Flowers by starting with an 8 ½-by-11-inch piece of paper folded in half crosswise.

- Make lots of Paper Flowers and tape or glue them to a large sheet of paper. Use felt-tip markers to add green stems and leaves and you have a flower mural.

# PRESSED FLOWERS

*Brigten up a winter window with these pretty flowers!*

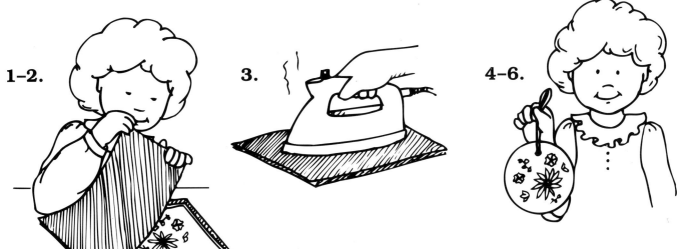

**1-2.**  **3.**  **4-6.**

**3.** Press around the edges of the stack with a medium-hot iron, then into the flat areas around the flowers to seal them inside.

**4.** Cut the pressing into a circle and punch a hole in the top.

**5.** Tie a piece of ribbon through the hole to make a loop.

**6.** Hang the Pressed Flowers in a window.

## YOU WILL NEED
- waxed paper
- paper towels
- fresh flowers
- iron
- scissors
- hole punch
- ribbon

**1.** Lay a piece of waxed paper on top of a paper towel, then make a flower arrangement on top of the waxed paper.

**2.** Lay another piece of waxed paper on top of the arrangement, then another paper towel.

## FOR MORE FUN
- Sprinkle some crayon shavings around the edges of the flowers before they are pressed. Your Pressed Flowers will be even more colorful.

*Adult supervision or assistance may be required.*

# MOUNTAIN SCULPTURE

*Make mountains out of this dough!*

1-4.    5-6.    7.

## YOU WILL NEED
- saucepan
- 1 cup cornstarch
- 2 cups baking soda
- 1⅓ cups warm water
- breadboard

**1.** In a saucepan, stir together the cornstarch and the baking soda.

**2.** Add the water and mix until smooth.

**3.** Bring the mixture to a boil over medium heat.

**4.** Stir until thick.

**5.** Pour the clay onto a breadboard to cool.

**6.** When the dough has cooled, knead it for two or three minutes.

**7.** Shape the dough into a mountain or a mountain range and let it dry.

## FOR MORE FUN
- Add color to your dough by kneading in food coloring or paint. Or paint your mountain after it dries.

- Use your Mountain Sculpture to retell the story, "The Bear and the Mountain." Be sure to make a bear cave.

*Adult supervision or assistance may be required.*

# SPONGE-PRINT MOUNTAIN SCENE

*Use your own sponge shapes to create a mountain scene!*

## YOU WILL NEED
- assorted colors of paint
- paintbrush
- piece of posterboard
- bear-shaped cookie cutter
- sponges
- pencil or pen
- scissors
- shallow containers

**1.** Paint a large mountain (or a mountain range) on a piece of posterboard. Let the paint dry.

**2.** Set a bear-shaped cookie cutter on top of a sponge, use a pencil or pen to trace around it, then cut out the bear shape.

**3.** Use scissors to cut sponges into tree shapes and flower shapes.

**4.** Pour paint into shallow containers.

**5.** Dip the tree shapes into paint and print trees all over the mountain.

**6.** Dip the flower shapes into paint and print flower shapes on the mountain.

**7.** Dip bear shapes into paint and add a few bears to your Mountain Scene.

## FOR MORE FUN
- Paint your Mountain Scene on a thin piece of paper. After it dries, tape the paper to a magnetic surface such as a baking sheet. Attach small magnets to the backs of the tree, bear, and flower shapes. Place the tree and flower shapes on the Mountain Scene and move the bears around however you like.

# BEAR SANDWICHES

## YOU WILL NEED
- large, heart-shaped cookie cutter
- whole-wheat bread
- knife
- peanut butter
- three raisins
- Maraschino cherry

**1.** Use a cookie cutter to cut heart shapes out of whole-wheat bread slices.

**2.** Use a knife to cut off the points of the hearts to make each one look like a bear face.

**3.** Spread peanut butter on your bear face.

**4.** Use raisins to make eyes and a mouth and a cherry to make a nose.

# BEAR BUFFET

## YOU WILL NEED
- honey
- peanut butter
- graham crackers
- berries
- chopped nuts
- banana slices

**1.** In a bowl, mix a little honey into some peanut butter.

**2.** Spread the honey-peanut butter mixture onto some graham crackers.

**3.** Top the graham crackers with some berries, chopped nuts, and banana slices before serving.

**FOR MORE FUN**
- Add some bear-shaped crackers to your Bear Buffet.

# BEAR GRAHAMS

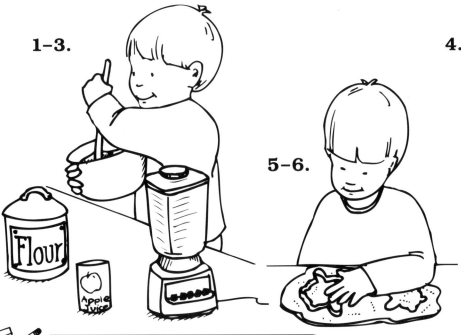

**1–3.**

**5–6.**

**4.**

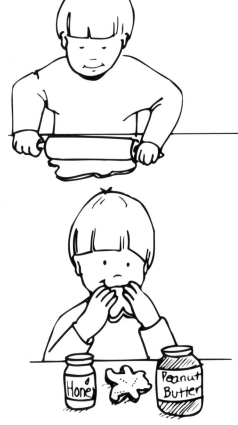

## YOU WILL NEED

- 1 cup graham flour
- 1 cup whole-wheat flour
- ½ teaspoon baking soda
- ½ teaspoon salt
- ¼ cup apple-juice concentrate
- ¼ cup vegetable oil
- 1 banana, sliced
- 1 teaspoon vanilla
- 1 teaspoon cinnamon

**1.** Stir flours, baking soda, and salt together in a large bowl.

**2.** Mix apple-juice concentrate, vegetable oil, banana, vanilla, and cinnamon in a blender.

**3.** Pour the wet ingredients into the dry ingredients. Stir until well mixed.

**4.** Roll out the dough on a floured surface until it is ⅛-inch thick.

**5.** Poke the dough with a fork, then use a cookie cutter to cut the dough into bear shapes.

**6.** Place the bear shapes on a baking sheet and bake at 350°F for 6 to 8 minutes.

**7.** Serve your Bear Graham Crackers with honey and peanut butter.

# The Bear and the Mountain

Sung to: "On Top of Old Smokey"

There once was a mountain
All covered with snow.
But in the summer
Wild flowers would grow.

The mountain was lonely,
He lived all alone.
He wished that someone
Could share his home.

At last came a friend,
A small little bear.
Who liked to wear flowers
In her soft, fuzzy hair.

The mountain was happy,
The bear was too,
Until the snows came,
Oh, what could she do?

"I'll make you a home,"
The mountain said,
"Where you can sleep
In a dry, warm bed."

The bear was so happy
With a friend and a home
That she never again
Decided to roam.

*Jean Warren*